Tick check

It is springtime in the beautiful state of Colorado. My roommate Jennifer went hiking, near where we live in Denver, Colorado. I took a nap then woke up to watch television in my boxers. When I heard a knock on the door and the beautiful voice of my sexy roommate Jennifer.

I said come on in Jennifer, what's up, she walked in with wet hair and a towel around her voluptuous body. She said can you do me a huge favor. I said sure, Jennifer said can you check my whole body for ticks. I usually have my boyfriend do this but since he is not around, you will have to do it for me.

I said sure no problem, Jennifer. She dropped her towel and wow, what a body Jennifer had on her. I was the happiest man in the state of Colorado. I started drooling first, I became erect second, third I started checking for ticks all over Jennifer's amazing beautiful body.

I held her big tits and checked them thoroughly. I checked every inch of her sweet white thighs. Jennifer bent over and I thoroughly checked out her amazing juicy ass. I checked and smelt her intoxicating white vagina. Finally, I massaged her head and found no ticks. She was happy to be tick free after a long hike.

Jennifer said thanks for checking my entire body for ticks. I said it was my pleasure to examine your lovely body. Jennifer said oh my god you have a huge tent in your pants. I said I'm looking at a sexy naked white girl, of course I'm hard, I'm not dead.

Jennifer laughed out loud. She said can I see it; I've never seen a black man's penis in my whole life. I said sure no problem, dropping my boxers for Jennifer's viewing pleasure. She said wow that is the most beautiful penis that I've seen in my life.

I smiled and said thank you. Jennifer said no wonder, your girlfriend Lindsay is over every weekend. I hear her moaning all the time several times during the weekend. I bet you give her many orgasms with that big beautiful cock of yours.

I said what can I say I love white pussy a lot and Lindsay loves getting fucked by my black cock.

Jennifer said I bet, too bad I'm not single, I'd love to see how many times you can make my white pussy come drilling me with your big black cock.

I said oh yeah that would be something to test out. Jennifer said I love listening to you fuck your girlfriend Lindsay on many occasions every weekend. I said does it turn you on and make your white pussy wet. She said oh yeah, I'm little perverted.

I love knowing that my love making has made you wet. Jennifer said I think one time you boned Lindsay 6 times in one weekend. I said wow you counted, Jennifer giggled and said yeah, I wanted to know and apparently, you don't have any problems getting it up. I said I have unlimited boners and Jennifer gave me the biggest smile ever.

Jennifer said thanks again for checking me for ticks then proceeded to hug me tight with her hot body. I held her tight and the hug lasted a long time with my black pole sliding between her sweet white thighs touching her white pussy.

I could feel the steam and moisture from her pussy on my cock shaft. Both of us were enjoying the hell out of our hug. Jennifer broke the hug then said I better go dry my hair. I will see you later, I said later hot Jennifer, she giggled and jiggled out of my room naked without her towel.

Monday, I came out for breakfast and Jennifer was wearing a thong, showing of her juicy ass and tank top that barely covered her big titties. I snuck up behind her and hugged her good morning. I kissed her neck and felt up her melons. Jennifer moaned and said good morning baby, how did you sleep. I said I slept well and she said I slept well too.

We ate breakfast together smiling and talking like close roommates. Jennifer hugged me and said have a good day at work and I said you too baby. When I came home, I relaxed on the couch. Jennifer came home and changed into a short skirt. She came and sat on my lap as I watched television.

I massaged her sweet white thighs and massaged her big tits as we watched television until dinner time. I went to sleep hot for Jennifer and I'm sure she was horny for me too.

Tuesday, I was in the shower when Jennifer came into my bathroom naked. I pulled her into the shower and soaped up every inch of her delicious body. Jennifer smiled the whole time. I gave her the soap and she soaped up my entire body. I really enjoyed her soaping up my hard cock for several minutes.

When we finished the showering, I dried Jennifer off and she dried me off too. We hugged naked good night and went to bed.

Wednesday morning, I went to the kitchen and Jennifer was totally naked preparing our breakfast. I took off my boxers and hugged her from behind with my full erection. Jennifer moaned and said do you like my outfit roomy. I said hell yeah. Jennifer reached behind and stroked my black cock. I rubbed her pussy as she stroked my cock, mostly concentrating on her clit.

Jennifer moaned when an orgasm hit her sexy body. I moaned five minutes later when I ejaculated on her juicy ass. Jennifer said that was fun. I cleaned my sperm off of her sweet white ass and the sperm that dripped down her sweet white thighs. Jennifer stroked my cock cleaning it, making sure that all the sperm came out of it. We sat down and ate breakfast naked giggling the whole time. We got ready for work then hugged each other goodbye with my hands all over Jennifer's big ass.

Thursday, I came home from work and Jennifer was on the couch totally naked. She said can you massage my back. I said sure taking all of my clothes off. I straddled Jennifer's juicy big ass with my hard cock between her cheeks. I massaged Jennifer's back as my hard-black cock slid between her wonderful ass.

Jennifer moaned oh god your massage feels so good thank you for doing this for me. I said my pleasure Jennifer. I massaged her back thoroughly until I was overwhelmed with pleasure. I ejaculated my warm sperm on Jennifer's back. I massaged my warm sperm unto Jennifer's sexy ass.

When I was done massaging her ass thoroughly. I said you better take a shower and get that sticky stuff of your great ass. She said thanks for the triple massage hugging me tight with my cock rubbing on her pussy and tits on my chest. I smacked her ass and said later sweet cheeks.

The weekend, my girlfriend Lindsay came over to spend the weekend. The first morning, we were in the kitchen talking when all of a sudden Lindsay said I really need to suck your cock right now. I said but Jennifer might walk in at any moment. Lindsay said I'm sure she's seen a white girl on her knees sucking a black man before that is when I said go for it suck away.

I held Lindsay's pretty black hair as she sucked my cock relentlessly. I said oh my god Lindsay I love your fucking mouth, it's so good for my cock. A minute into my blowjob from Lindsay, Jennifer walked in and said sorry guys. I need some coffee really badly.

Lindsay stopped and said you can stay for breakfast. I don't mind you seeing me blow my boyfriend's mind. Jennifer giggled and said wow that's a big black cock, I'm so impressed that you can suck his big dick. Lindsay said I've had a lot of practice sucking his big dick. I said my girlfriend is the best cocksucker in all of Colorado. Jennifer giggled then I moaned with pleasure ejaculating into Lindsay's wonderful mouth.

Lindsay swallowed it down like breakfast and with ease. Jennifer said oh my god did you just swallow his sperm. Lindsay said oh yeah, I love doing it for my man, it blows his mind every time. Jennifer laughed out loud. I said I love it every time she swallows my warm seed.

We all sat and ate breakfast together. Later, Lindsay and I were in my bedroom when she said, do you think Jennifer's pussy was wet from me sucking and swallowing your sperm. I said probably, I know it turned me on with her watching us fool around. Lindsay said I wonder if she has had any black cock inside her white vagina.

I said no and I told Lindsay about me checking Jennifer's naked body for ticks after her hiking trip. That is when Lindsay came up with a plan to seduce Jennifer. All three of us were on the couch later the next night, Jennifer said I'm tired, I'll turn in for the evening.

Lindsay kissed me passionately after Jennifer left then said let's do it baby. Lindsay took off her nightgown and I took off my boxers. I spread Lindsay's sweet white thighs, kissing every inch of them, then I moved on to her pink slit. I licked it real good fingering her pussy. I started chewing on her clit and it drove her while with passion.

Lindsay held my head and thoroughly enjoyed my tongue lashing of her pussy. She said time to fuck baby I need your big stick in my white vagina. I didn't hesitate, I plunged my love dagger into my woman. I started massaging her pussy with my love stick in the most wonderful of ways.

I saw Jennifer watching me fuck my girlfriends tight little cunt. Lindsay said oh yeah, my stud boyfriend I love your big dick and all the orgasms that you give me when you pound me.

Lindsay moaned and gave up the lubrication on my cock, I bent her over away from Jennifer. I impaled her again on my good wood. I smacked her juicy ass and took her hard. She came and came so many times that I lost track. I got that wonderful feeling and ejaculated into Lindsay's inviting vagina.

The next weekend, somehow Lindsay got Jennifer to watch television in our bed. Lindsay asked Jennifer if she minded if we boned. Jennifer said I don't mind go for it. I said cool, I mounted Lindsay, since she was stroking my cock and I was fingering her pussy under the covers as we watched television.

Jennifer watched as I massaged Lindsay's white vagina with my black penis over and over. Lindsay moaned oh god yeah, I love your big fucking cock always making me cream. I bent Lindsay over smacking her juicy big ass with my cock before penetrating her and pulling her long black hair.

I started pounding her harder and harder. Lindsay moaned louder and louder giving up the cream on the cock. Jennifer said oh yeah white girl, take that big black cock deep in your little white pussy. Lindsay giggled and said oh yeah, I love taking it from my big black stud. I moaned oh yeah, my tight Lindsay releasing all of my pleasure from my balls deep in her tight little cunt.

Lindsay turned around and kissed me passionately while I massaged her juicy booty. Jennifer said wow that was hot, live porn. Lindsay and I said you're welcome Jennifer. Lindsay said I'm going to sleep, getting the shit fucked out of you is very tiring. Jennifer laughed out loud. Lindsay went to sleep. Jennifer said I better go to my room. I held her hand and said please don't go Jennifer.

She said ok baby I'll stay, I said there is plenty of room. We turned off the television and tried to go to sleep. I massaged Jennifer's sweet white thighs, she said oh my god you're so bad, you naughty man. I said you know you like it. Jennifer said I do like it, I'm horny, I spooned her after lifting up her nightgown.

I kissed her neck and she moaned. I whispered let me stick my black penis in your white vagina.

Jennifer said your girlfriend Lindsay is right there, she might wake up and I said she is a sound sleeper, she never wakes up for anything, not even the smoke alarm. Jennifer said wow really. I said yeah, so what do you say, Jennifer said I love missionary with the man on top so get on top and see if you can get that big black cock in my little white pussy.

I mounted Jennifer and forcefully penetrated her white pussy with my black penis. Jennifer smiled and I kissed her. She said oh wow I can't believe your black cock is in my white pussy and your girlfriend is right there sleeping. I said oh yeah so exciting. I started fucking Jennifer slowly. She held me tight as I gave it to her. She moaned with pleasure as we fucked in unison. I said I love your tight ass vagina. Jennifer said I love your big black penis deep inside my white cunt.

Jennifer moaned oh god yeah as she came on my cock. I could feel my cock getting more lube from her vagina on it. I started fucking Jennifer harder and she moaned more and more. She said oh yeah baby, I felt cream after cream on my cock as I fucked Jennifer. I felt my balls tighten and I filled Jennifer with my warm sperm.

We kissed each other passionately. I said double cream pies, Jennifer giggled then said thanks for giving me my first black cock. I said my pleasure, I've wanted to hit that for a long time. Jennifer said I've wanted you to spread my white thighs and have your way with me for a while now.

I woke up to my sexy girlfriend Lindsay and my sexy horny roommate Jennifer. I said good morning ladies, I hope you both slept well. Jennifer said I slept well and Lindsay said I slept like a baby. Jennifer left and went to her bedroom. Lindsay said did you fuck her with your dirty cock from my pussy last night. I said oh yeah and she wanted it too. Lindsay said oh wow double cream pies. I said best night ever with two hot white bitches. Lindsay laughed out loud, we put on our robes and went out to eat breakfast.

Jennifer was feeling really good and looking at me. She smiled the whole breakfast and so did Lindsay for different lustful reasons. After Lindsay left, I took a shower and then went to bed. I felt a warm sensation on my cock, I woke up and it was my horny roommate Jennifer. I said hey sexy that feels good don't stop. Jennifer's blow job game was second to none and before I knew it. I was ejaculating warm sperm into Jennifer's wonderful mouth of pleasure.

I said thanks for the blow job, Jennifer said my pleasure, I've been dying to suck your dick and swallow for a while, just like your girlfriend says that you like. I smiled and said thank you baby. I said my turn baby, I threw her onto the bed, kissing every inch of her sweet white thighs. I licked her pink slit up and down as she moaned with pleasure. I latched onto her clit and inserted my middle finger into Jennifer's tasty vagina. Jennifer moaned like crazy as I fingered her pussy really fast and sucked the hell out of her clit. I felt Jennifer's body stiffen and she scream oh god that is the spot as an orgasm overwhelmed her hot steamy body.

I lay beside Jennifer smiling when she said you are the best roommate ever in terms of pleasure and satisfaction. I said thank you for the kind words sweet Jennifer with a peck on the lips. Lindsay texted me because, she was watching on our mutual webcams, saying how hot it was to see me eating Jennifer's pussy and her sucking my black dick until we both came.

When Jennifer went to sleep, I texted Lindsay back and sent her naked pictures of Jennifer and me in bed together. Jennifer's boyfriend called her cell phone, so I woke her up to answer it. She woke up and answered it, I messed with her by sucking on her big titties. Then I had an idea to tit fuck her while she talked to her boyfriend. I held her white melons and slid my black cock between them over and over. The contrast was intoxicating and erotic. Jennifer was smiling the whole time as she talked to her boyfriend. The conversation went on for a while and it help me a lot. I felt the great urge so I ejaculated all over her melons. Jennifer's eyes and mouth doubled in size as I massaged my warm sperm into her melons.

When Jennifer finished talking on the phone with her boyfriend, I told her that we needed to go grocery shopping. We both put on shorts and a t-shirt. Jennifer's were a whole lot sexier and tighter than my loose-fitting summer outfit.

I was walking behind Jennifer when I told her that her ass looks amazing in those short tight jeans. Jennifer said thanks baby. We were in the aisle alone. I looked around then smacked her juicy ass. Jennifer moaned and said you're going to make me wet. I said it's my job to keep the hot white bitch wet. Jennifer laughed out loud. She hugged and kissed me in public. I didn't miss the opportunity to feel on her big ass.

We were checking out when the cashier Amanda asked if we are a couple. I said I love fucking her tight white pussy and Jennifer said I love his big black cock ejaculating inside of me. Amanda said a horny couple, I like it. We both smiled at her, she said can I hug you guys. I said sure, she hugged Jennifer then it was my turn. I hugged Amanda and she moaned oh yeah, it's hard, that is what I was hoping for and Jennifer giggled.

I massaged Amanda's big ass then she gave me a peck on the lips. She said that is to remember me by, Jennifer and I left to go home. I said wow that was hot with the cashier. Jennifer said I bet she would let you fuck her. I said oh yeah, she let me feel on her big ass and she kissed me. I'd say that is safe to assume that she would let be stick my black penis inside her horny little white cunt.

I'm glad that I slipped her my business card into the back pocket of her tight pants. I didn't expect to hear from her and I didn't until I was hiring for a new secretary. Amanda walked in for the interview in a short red skirt and tight white shirt with no bra hiding her melons. I said hi Amanda, it's great to see you again. She hugged me tight and then she kissed me passionately. I reached up her skirt to massage her bare ass.

Amanda said I hope I can be your secretary. I said let's do the interview and find out, everything looks good so far as I read over her resume. I conducted the interview and Amanda was right for the job. I said your hired when can you start. She said I have to give the store two weeks' notice before I can start working for my dream boss. I smiled at her and she smiled back at me.

I said great, I'll see you in two weeks then. Amanda and I hugged and kissed goodbye. I informed HR that I was hiring Amanda, they got all the paperwork ready.

I went home to Jennifer and told her that I hired the waitress to be my secretary. Jennifer said I know that you're going to fuck her white pussy. I said you know it. Lindsay came to my job to meet

Amanda before I fucked her. They were hugging and it really turned me on. I told Amanda that this was my girlfriend Lindsay. She said it was a pleasure meeting you Lindsay as she left.

Afterwards, Amanda said so who was the other white girl that you are fucking that came to the store with you. I said that is my roommate Jennifer, Amanda said does your girlfriend know your fucking her too. I said yeah but Jennifer doesn't know that my girlfriend knows that I'm fucking her. Amanda said wow so kinky. I kissed Amanda and smacked her juicy ass, I said back to work sweet cheeks. She said yes boss and jiggled back to work.

A week later, I told Amanda that she was coming home with me tonight. She called her mom Amy and told her that she was spending the night with her boss. We stripped naked when I got home and I laid down, Amanda started sucking my cock as Lindsay watched her blow on my pleasure stick.

Amanda slid down my black pole as I squeezed her big fucking titties. I moaned as Amanda rode my black pole giving herself a lot of pleasure. I moaned oh Amanda, I've been wanting you on my cock for weeks now. She said same here baby, I was hoping that you would let me ride your big black cock. I said do you like it baby. Amanda said oh yeah, my white pussy has never felt better.

Jennifer came into my room totally naked. She said sorry I didn't know that you had company. Amanda said stay don't go Jennifer. She came in and watched as Amanda fucked me. I bent Amanda over and pulled her long black hair. I fucked her hard as Jennifer and Lindsay watched. Amanda moaned oh god I love getting fucked while your girlfriend watches naked. I moaned oh god as I ejaculated inside of Amanda for the first time.

Jennifer smacked her ass and said do you like taking my boyfriend's warm sperm. Amanda said oh yeah especially with his hot girlfriend watching.

I lay between them holding hands. Jennifer kissed me and stroked my cock. Five minutes later, I was hard again. Amanda said wow hard again now that is a productive dick. Jennifer said my turn holding my dick and sliding down. I held her tits as she rode me hard. She leaned down to kiss me as Lindsay and Amanda watched. I felt Jennifer moisturizing my cock with her first orgasm then her second. I bent her over and took her from behind. Amanda smacked her ass and said take it all you little slut. Jennifer moaned and took all of me repeatedly. Amanda kissed me passionately causing me to ejaculate inside of Jennifer's tight little cunt.

I kissed Amanda and Jennifer as we lay back relaxing before they drifted off to sleep. I took a picture and sent it to Lindsay to put on her wall of pleasure in big print. When the morning came, I woke both of my sexy lovers up and told them it was time to shower.

All three of us walked into my shower naked holding each other. I soaped up Amanda's sexy naked body focusing on her big tits, juicy ass, sweet white thighs and pussy. Jennifer soaped up my body thoroughly then focused on my hard cock.

Amanda and I both soaped up Jennifer's hot body. I hope that Lindsay was watching on our mutual shower cam. Jennifer was all smiles as Amanda and I soaped up her big tits, big ass, sweet white thighs and her pussy. Amanda and Jennifer knelt before me licking my shaft then both of them took turns sucking my black bone thoroughly. The pleasure was immense and then both of them started sucking my cock head at the same time. I lost it and ejaculated into both of their mouths at the same time and they both swallowed. I said wow that was amazing. Both Jennifer and Amanda said you're welcome.

Jennifer said look at the time, we need to get to work. We dried each other off quickly. I took Amanda home to change. I was waiting when her mom Amy came out in a little tiny robe. She said you must be Amanda's new boss. I said I am her new boss. Amy hugged me tight and I couldn't help but squeezed her big ass. She said oh wow you're a friendly one, she French kissed me and pulled me on top of her on the couch. She opened the robe and she was naked under it. Amy unzipped my fly and fished my cock out. I slammed it up her wet cunt and started fucking Amy really hard and fast. Amy moaned oh god sir we just met and your big cock is already making me cum. I felt a great amount of lubrication on my cock from Amy. I fucked her harder and harder as she held me tight.

Amanda came out and said oh my god boss you're balls deep inside of my mom we are going to be so late. I said oh god just a second Amanda. I moaned and filled Amanda's mom with some fresh breakfast cream curtesy of my black sausage. I kissed Amy and said that was wonderful mam thank you so much for the warm welcome. She said my pleasure stud. Amanda said let's go boss. I put my dick away and left Amy all smiles on the couch and my warm sperm oozing out of her horny white pussy.

Amanda and I walked to the car. I said where is your dad, Amanda said upstairs sleeping. I said oh wow your mom is a horny little slut. Amanda said now you know where I got it from and I laughed out loud. We went to work and walked into our building straight to our offices with 2 minutes to spare.

A few days later when I came home from work. Jennifer met me at the door totally naked and horny as hell. She took my briefcase put it down, took me by the hand to my bedroom. Jennifer unzipped my fly and took my hard cock out. She said fuck me in your suit my stud. I said sure honey.

Jennifer laid back ready for her favorite position. I mounted her and plunged my love dagger into the heart of her pleasure. She moaned as I gave it to her, she said I love my horny roommate. I said I love you too, Jennifer. I fucked her harder and harder. It was intense fucking her with my work clothes on. Jennifer fucking loved it; I showed her pussy no mercy hammering away at her pussy. My whole cock and balls felt flooded with cream from Jennifer, god knows how many times she had come so far.

Jennifer said I'm addicted to your big black cock, I smiled and moaned as I filled her with my love. We held each other and kissed, Lindsay came into my room, she said you dirty little white whore you like my boyfriend's big black cock. I said oh no and Jennifer said oh crap don't hurt me. Lindsay came at Jennifer and she curled up into the fetal position with her eyes closed. Lindsay and I started laughing and Jennifer opened her eyes. We both said gotcha.

The end

www.ingramcontent.com/pod-product-compliance
Lightning Source LLC
LaVergne TN
LVHW020547160826
845677LV00015B/4252

9798355590475